Polly watched in horror as Sam's blond head sank into the dirt.

Audrey was shrieking, and Polly wanted to do the same. Instead, she grabbed Sam's feet, which now were the only part of him showing.

"Get out, Audrey," Polly shouted. "Run!"

Audrey didn't move. She just watched with wide eyes.

Polly braced her feet as the dirt in the old foundation began to move in a circle, like a giant whirlpool.

The last thing Polly saw was Audrey's open mouth as the dirt swept Audrey's feet out from under her. Then Polly felt a small hand catch her ankle, and she, too, sank into the earth.

Earth Magic

THE SECOND BOOK IN
The Magic Elements Quartet

by Mallory Loehr

A Stepping Stone Book™

RANDOM HOUSE 🏠 NEW YORK

ACKNOWLEDGMENTS

Thanks to Jim Thomas and Kate Klimo for their support,

Cathy Goldsmith for a super design, Elizabeth Miles for fabulous covers,

Mary Pope Osborne for her encouragement,

and one of my best pals, Audrey Ellzey,

for lending her name to a character who only vaguely resembles her.

www.randomhouse.com/kids

Library of Congress Cataloging-in-Publication Data
Loehr, Mallory.
Earth magic : magic elements quartet / by Mallory Loehr.—1st ed.
p.   cm. — "Book two." "A Stepping Stone book."
SUMMARY: While visiting their grandparents' farm, Polly and Sam and their
young cousin are drawn to an unusual rock that seems to want their help.
ISBN 0-679-89218-4 (trade) — ISBN 0-679-99218-9 (lib. bdg.)
[1. Brothers and sisters—Fiction.   2. Mythology, Greek—Fiction.]   I. Title.
PZ7.L82615Ear   1999   [Fic]—dc21   99-43276

Printed in the United States of America November 1999 10 9 8 7 6 5 4 3 2 1

Random House, Inc.   New York, Toronto, London, Sydney, Auckland

RANDOM HOUSE and colophon are registered trademarks and
A STEPPING STONE BOOK and colophon are trademarks of Random House, Inc.

For my grandparents—
Grandmother Mimi and
"Plain Old" Grandmother & Grandfather—
wise, wonderful, and amazing people!

Contents

Earth
Magic

Prologue

She saw them through her many eyes. They were humans, and old enough to help. She watched them awhile, and she could see that there was something special about them— something that made them different. They were the right ones.

The mother gathered her magic and wrapped it around her child like a blanket. Maybe this time she wouldn't have to be alone again. Maybe this time winter wouldn't come.

Far under the ground, a three-headed dog howled...

CHAPTER ONE

Earth Child

There was nothing strange about the rock. Nothing—except that it popped up out of nowhere in front of Polly's creeping feet.

Polly fell headlong onto the mossy ground. Her younger brother, Sam, was so close behind her that he tripped over the rock, too, and landed on top of her.

"Get off me," Polly said, her voice muffled by moss.

"Sorry," said Sam.

He scrambled to his feet.

Polly sat up and glared at the lumpy rock.

"Where did *that* come from?" she asked.

She looked around the woods accusingly. Many of the trees were still green. It was the beginning of November, but fall was very late this year.

"I swear it came out of nowhere," she said.

"You shouldn't swear," said Sam.

"Oh, you know what I mean," Polly said.

Sam looked at her with wide, innocent eyes.

"Now, where were we?" said Polly.

"We were just escaping the evil robot water rats," said Sam.

"That's right," said Polly. "I remember." She paused to think. "Okay. Let's just say they're far behind us now."

She had begun to climb to her feet when she let out a little gasp.

"Are you hurt?" asked Sam.

"No," said Polly. She was staring at something beside her.

"What?" asked Sam. "What is it?"

"I think…" said Polly. "I think…maybe… it's more magic!"

Sam dropped to his knees and peered around his sister.

Wedged under the rock was something that looked like a grayish brown piece of paper. It was folded into a strange shape and was speckled with green, moldy-looking spots.

"It almost looks like a rock or a funny mushroom," said Sam.

Polly slowly reached her hand out, as if the paper were a wild animal that would disappear if she moved too quickly. She pulled gently on it to see if the corner would come loose. It didn't move. Polly was too eager to see what might be inside to waste time. She settled for carefully undoing the folds. The paper felt like soft, soft cloth.

Inside, the paper was light brown with grass and flowers embedded in it. Its edges were like a ragged leaf. Curly brown writing only a shade darker than the paper covered the page. The uneven light in the woods made it hard to read.

"Another parchment," breathed Sam. He reached out and touched the soft page.

A sudden gust of wind blew through the woods. The world rustled around Sam and Polly. Sunlight and shadow played across the paper as the breeze shook the leaves overhead.

"I can't read it," said Sam.

"Me neither," said Polly. "Wait until the wind dies down."

They both held their breath and watched the shadows on the parchment slowly dance to a halt.

Sam leaned in and peered at the parchment, his nose almost touching its surface.

"You are way too close," said Polly. "You won't be able to read it like that."

"But I can't read it from farther away, either," said Sam.

"Maybe if we get it out from under the rock," said Polly.

"It looks really stuck," said Sam.

Polly tried to free the paper again. This

time when she pulled, it felt as if someone be-neath the rock were holding tight to it. Polly shook her head at the silly idea.

"Pull harder," said Sam.

Polly did. "I don't want to rip it," she said.

But it was too late. The parchment was torn, a corner of the page remaining beneath the rock.

Polly tilted the parchment back and forth. Sam watched. Funnily enough, shade seemed to make the faint writing stand out more than sunlight did. In the sunlight, the letters hid be-hind the grass and flowers in the paper.

Polly turned until the paper was com-pletely in shade. Sam turned with her.

"Magic, all right," Polly said with a grin as the words floated dimly to the surface of the page.

Sam sighed happily. "I knew it would hap-pen again. What's it say?"

Sam closed his eyes to listen more carefully as Polly slowly read the words on the paper out loud.

Thank you for watching my Earth Child.
Keep my little one always in your sight.
In an emergency, please call.
The following elemental objects
can be used for communication
(each can be used only once):
The soft skin of the forest floor.
The tiny seed of the mightiest tree.
ella of the mouse.

"'Ella of the mouse'?" said Sam. "What's that?"

"It's where the stupid paper tore," said Polly.

"Oh," said Sam.

"They sound like riddles to me," said Polly. "At least we have all of the first two. Maybe we won't have to use the third one."

"I bet we will," said Sam. "We've never baby-sat anyone except ourselves before."

"And exactly *what* are we baby-sitting?" Polly asked.

"An Earth Child," said Sam.

"I know that," said Polly. "But what is an Earth Child?"

"Oh," said Sam. "I see what you mean."

They looked at the parchment again. Polly read the words out loud, Sam looking over her shoulder.

"There aren't any clues there," said Polly. "Do you see any?"

She looked at Sam. He looked stumped, too.

"Maybe it's an element thing?" Sam suggested.

"Well, we have to figure it out," Polly said. "We can't just let the magic go."

Sam shook his head vigorously. "No way."

"It's something that has something to do with an element," said Polly. "Elements are water, earth, air, and fire. You know, like the magic from the summer. That was all about the water element. So maybe this is about one of the other ones. But which one?"

They looked back at the parchment.

Polly ran her finger along the words. Her

finger stopped on one of them. "Forest," she said.

"Maybe it's fire!" Sam suggested. "Forest *fire*. They go together."

Polly moved her finger along the words again. She stopped on "tree."

"Tree," she said.

"Tree fire?" said Sam.

Polly's finger kept going. She came to the end of the parchment and tapped the word "mouse."

"I don't know about the mouse," she said. "But trees and forests sound like earth things."

"Yeah," said Sam. "But fire would be neat." When he was younger, he had gotten in trouble for lighting matches. Even now that he knew better, fire was still interestingly mysterious to him.

Polly began pacing fiercely back and forth, kicking up leaves. Sam stopped thinking about fire and paced with her, trying to look as fierce.

"Trees?" Polly muttered. "Grass? Flowers? Worms?"

"I could baby-sit a worm," Sam said hope-fully. "Or maybe that's why it says 'mouse.' Maybe we have to take care of a mouse."

Polly thought for a minute. "I don't think so," she said. "It would be too easy." She loved a challenge.

"Finding and catching a mouse wouldn't be easy," said Sam.

Polly shook her head. "I don't think that's it. Now be quiet while I'm thinking."

She looked up, hoping it would help her get an idea. The trees seemed to be bending down toward them.

A breeze blew.

The leaves made a whispering sound.

Light slanted through the trees.

And Polly tripped over the rock *again*.

Sam fell right on top of her *again*.

"Darn rock!" growled Polly.

Sam started laughing. Then Polly started laughing, too. Soon they both were laughing and rolling on the ground.

Slowly, they calmed down. With a giggly

gulp, Polly opened her eyes. Not an inch from her nose was the lumpy rock.

"Sam," she said, "I swear this rock is moving around."

"Don't swear," Sam giggled.

"No, really," said Polly.

Sam tried to make a serious face. Polly kept staring at the rock.

"What if…" she began. "What if…*this rock is the Earth Child?*"

Sam's silliness fell away. He looked at the lumpy rock through new eyes.

Polly looked at the parchment. She read the words again.

"What else could the Earth Child be?" she asked.

Dappled light played over the rock. The trees leaned in closer.

Sam reached out and touched the bumpy surface of the rock. It was cool and smooth over the lumpiness.

"We'll take care of you," he said softly.

Polly reached out and touched it, too. It felt

like a rock to her. But it *had* to be the Earth Child.

"I've never had to baby-sit anyone before," she said. "You don't count. Mom says I can baby-sit for real when I'm twelve. But that's not for two more years."

Suddenly, Polly wasn't sure that she wanted to baby-sit ever. Although it *would* be nice to make some money. Baby-sitters made a lot of money, at least five dollars an hour. But they wouldn't be getting paid for taking care of an Earth Child. Or was being in a world of magic like being paid, but in a different way?

Sam's voice broke into her thoughts.

"Maybe Grandma will help," he said.

"Yeah," said Polly. "Either that or she'll think we're crazy."

Sam nodded. "It *is* a little crazy," he said, "if you don't know about magic."

Polly nodded. "I'm so glad we do."

"Me too," said Sam.

"Well, if we have to not let it out of our sight, then we have to figure out a way to get it back to the farmhouse," said Polly. "Let's roll it over."

"There might be bugs under there," said Sam. "That's what's usually under big rocks."

"I hope not," said Polly. "I hate bugs."

They both pushed the rock, but it wouldn't budge.

"Let's try the other side," suggested Polly.

They went to the other side. They pushed as hard as they could, but the rock still wouldn't move.

"It shouldn't be this hard," said Polly. "It's not *that* big."

"Let's dig under it," suggested Sam.

So they each took a side and began digging. And digging. And digging.

"This rock isn't so small after all," said Polly.

Finally, each of them reached the bottom edge. The rock was about eight inches longer than it had seemed from above.

"It's like an iceberg," said Sam as he curled his fingers underneath the rock.

"Pull," said Polly.

They pulled until their fingers slipped.

"Ouch," said Sam, rubbing his hands.

"We had better figure this out fast," said Polly. "It's going to be dark soon."

Sam looked around. He hadn't even noticed the light fading. They were visiting their grandparents' farm, and the rule there was that kids could play outside as long as it was light.

"I think we're going to have to call for help," Sam said.

CHAPTER TWO

First Emergency

Polly scrunched up her face in thought. "I think you're right," she said.

She picked up the paper from under the tree. "'The tiny seed of the mightiest tree,'" she mused.

"Isn't that a saying or a quote or something?" asked Sam.

"Yeah," said Polly. "Mighty trees from little somethings grow."

"I know—trees grow from seeds!" said Sam.

Polly rolled her eyes. "Of course they grow from seeds. But we have to know what *kind* of seed."

Now it was Sam's turn to roll his eyes. "A *tree* seed. *Duh.*"

"Hellooo," said Polly. "Some tree seeds have names. You know, like those whirly things that come from maples."

"What are those called?" said Sam. He hated it when Polly made him feel dumb. "I bet you don't know."

"I don't," Polly admitted.

Sam felt a little better. "Can we give up on this one?" he said.

"Okay," said Polly, looking back at the parchment. "Then we have to figure out what 'the soft skin of the forest floor' is."

"'Soft skin of the forest floor'?" said Sam. "I don't see any skin."

"It's like the Earth Child thing," said Polly. "We have to make the right connection." She thought for a minute. "The ground is like the woods' skin. The trees are like giant hairs."

"Oh," said Sam, "I get it. And that makes us like giant fleas!"

"Be serious," said Polly. "I can't do all the thinking around here."

Sam made a serious, thinking face.

"Okay," said Polly. "How about dirt? Or fallen leaves—they make a kind of skin."

"Uh-huh," said Sam, "but they're not really soft. Unless you put lotion on them." He laughed at his own joke.

"Stop being silly," said Polly. "We both have to take care of this rock! You have to help."

"Right," said Sam soberly.

"Get down and look at the ground for ideas," Polly said. She folded the parchment back up and put it in her pocket. They both got down on their hands and knees.

The light had gone from gold to gray, and it was hard to see.

Sam called out the names of things he felt as he reached across the ground.

"Sticks!…Pebbles!…Dirt!…Cobwebs!… Moss!"

"Too pointy!…Too bumpy!…Too dirty!… Too sticky!…Too—What did you say?" Polly asked.

"Moss!" exclaimed Sam, holding up a handful of soft greenery.

"That's it!" said Polly. "You got it!"

"I did?" said Sam. He looked at his handful of moss. "Yeah, I did! Now what do we do with it?"

"It just says we can use it to call," said Polly.

"But that's like saying it's a phone," said Sam. "How can we use it to call? And who are we calling?"

"I have an idea," said Polly. She took the clump of moss from Sam's hand and carefully tore it in two. Then she held half of it against her ear like a phone. The other half she talked into.

"Hello," she said into the mossy telephone in her most grown-up voice. "I'm trying to reach the Earth Child's parent or guardian, please. This is the baby-sitter calling."

There was the sound of leaves rustling in

the wind. But there wasn't any wind.

The rustling grew louder.

Sam and Polly looked at each other, eyes wide. Polly's hands dropped to her sides, still clutching the moss.

Then the rustling became words. *Please leave a message,* the leafy voice said.

Polly took a deep breath and collected her thoughts. "Well," she said, "this is kind of an emergency."

"Yeah," Sam called. "We have to get back to the farmhouse, but we can't get the rock—um, I mean, the Earth Child—up. And we'll be in big trouble if we don't get back very soon."

"Yes," said Polly. "So can someone please do something about it immediately? Or we may have to leave the rock—I mean, the Earth Child—behind, and I don't know what will happen if we do that."

Yesssss, rustled the leaves. *Immediately.*

"Oh," said Polly. "Great. Thanks."

She shrugged her shoulders at Sam. He shrugged back.

"Guess we have to wait," she said.

Polly and Sam waited, watching the sky turn violet-pink. A few stars began to twinkle. There was no moon yet.

Suddenly, the ground heaved beneath them.

"What—" said Sam. He stumbled back against a tree.

Polly stumbled after him. They held on to the tree, which was also moving, as dirt swirled around the rock.

The ground looked as if it was boiling with snakes!

Polly screamed. Then Sam screamed, too.

The snakes writhed and twitched and thrashed about. They also seemed to be pushing the rock up, out of its firm bed.

The tree rocked. Sam and Polly rocked with it. Suddenly, Polly realized that what she was looking at wasn't snakes at all, but tree roots.

"It's the roots," she said.

Sam opened his eyes. He looked at the

roots and his expression changed. "Whew."

And then it was over. The tree stopped rocking, and the roots slithered back under the forest floor. The rock sat, ready and waiting.

Now Sam and Polly became aware of another sound, the sound of Grandpa's tractor.

"Sam! Polly!" they heard him calling over the growling engine.

They dug their fingers under the rock and just managed to lift it. They staggered about a bit, getting their balance.

Polly looked at the hole where the rock had been. But she didn't see the torn corner of the magic note with the missing words.

Against the last light of the sunset, they could see the silhouette of the tractor and their grandfather's Santa Claus shape. The tractor stopped, and the engine switched off. Then the headlights switched on.

"GRANDPA!" Polly and Sam shouted.

"And not a moment too soon," came their grandfather's booming voice. "I can tell your grandma that you were with me before dark."

Sam and Polly staggered forward, carrying the rock between them.

"Now, what have we here?" said Grandpa. "Rock collecting, are you? Can't you find something a little smaller?"

"No, sir," said Sam. "We have to have this one."

"If you must have it, then I'll lend you a hand," said Grandpa. "Here, let me take it." He stretched out his arms and bent his knees.

"But you just hurt your back!" said Polly. "Grandma said you weren't allowed to lift anything heavy."

Grandpa sighed and straightened up. "You sound just like your grandmother," he said, "and you're right. It's not too much farther. We'll put it in the hay cart."

They walked toward the lights of the little red tractor. Hitched to the back of the tractor was a small cart filled with hay. Grandpa climbed into the tractor's seat.

As gently as they could, Polly and Sam put the rock in the cart. They pushed the rock into the hay and then climbed in beside it. The dry smell of hay surrounded them.

The tractor engine started.

"Hang on!" shouted Grandpa. "We're off to dinner!"

Sam and Polly gripped the sides of the cart as it lurched forward. Then they lay back in the hay and looked up at the sky as more and more stars came out like fireflies.

CHAPTER THREE

❀❀❀❀❀❀❀❀❀

Rock Around the Clock

The tractor rumbled into the valley of the Farm, where the four fields met.

Polly always thought that from a distance the Farm looked just like a giant cushion with a big button sewn in the middle. The fields were cut in half one way by a gravel road and the other way by a small stream.

The tractor bumped onto the gravel road and crossed the stream with a splash. Then it reluctantly climbed the hill to where the farmhouse and the barn sat, one on either side of the road. It wasn't a real farm with fields of wheat or corn. But there were chickens, rabbits, and a big vegetable garden, and once Grandpa had planted a field with soybeans as an experiment.

Sam and Polly were visiting their grandparents' farm for a long weekend. They had never been there without their parents before. And here it was, only their first day, and already something wonderful had happened!

The tractor pulled up beside the house.

"Hop off," called Grandpa. "I've got to put the horse and carriage away."

Sam and Polly pushed the rock to the edge of the cart. Then they jumped out. The tractor lurched forward.

"Stop! Stop!" they shouted.

Grandpa looked back. Then he put on the brake.

"I forgot about your collection!" he laughed.

Carefully, Sam and Polly pulled the rock off the cart. Carrying it between them, they staggered over the lawn to the lit porch of the farmhouse.

"What on earth have you kids got?" their grandmother said, holding the door open.

Sam and Polly wobbled toward the door.

"It's a rock, Grandma," said Sam. "A big rock! And it's really an Earth Child."

Polly gave Sam the "don't say too much" look.

"I can see that," said Grandma. "But I think the rock will be happier outside, where it belongs."

"We have to put it down for a second," said Polly.

Carefully, they lowered the rock to the edge of the porch.

"I think it will be very happy right there," said Grandma.

"But we need to really watch it," Polly protested. "We're taking care of it."

"I'll help!" piped up a little voice.

Polly and Sam looked at each other as a little head appeared behind their grandmother. It was covered with curly dark hair that fell into a pair of electric blue eyes.

"Look who's here," said Grandma. "Your aunt dropped Audrey off for the weekend while you guys were out in the woods."

"Wonderful!" said their grandfather as he came across the lawn. "The more, the merrier!"

Sam and Polly nodded weakly.

"I just turned six," Audrey announced.

"Wow," said Polly. "That's big."

Audrey nodded, her curls bouncing. "I can help you with the rock," she said. "Because I am six now."

"I'm sure you can," said Polly, smiling sweetly. Audrey was *always* helpful.

Their grandmother gave Polly a look.

"Well, come on in, everyone," said Grandma. "Dinner's waiting."

"But the rock—" began Polly.

"We'll talk about it over dinner," Grandpa said.

Sam and Polly looked at each other. It was not good to argue with grandparents. Polly didn't know what to do. They *had* to bring the rock inside.

"Um, Grandma," Polly said. "It's really important to me to bring the rock in. We aren't supposed to let it out of our sight."

Now it was Grandma and Grandpa's turn to exchange a look. They smiled at each other, and Grandpa gave a little nod, his eyes twinkling.

"All right," Grandma said, "but you'll have to wash the dirt off first."

"In the bathtub?" Sam asked.

"I'll pull the hose over for you," said Grandpa.

"But that might be too cold for the Earth Child!" Polly said, shivering at the thought.

"Rock children survive all sorts of things," Grandma said with a smile. "And your dinner is getting cold while we talk about it. You two hurry up, and we'll start dinner without you."

"I'll help!" said Audrey.

"No, Audrey," said Grandma, "you are coming in for dinner."

"But I want to help Sam and Polly!" said Audrey, her lower lip sticking out.

"You can help tomorrow," said Grandma.

"Okay," said Audrey.

Tomorrow? Sam and Polly looked at each other in horror. After Grandma and Audrey had gone inside, Polly said, "We'll take care of it tomorrow. She can't tag along everywhere. Taking care of one child is enough."

Grandpa had dragged the hose over from the pump.

"I'll turn it on!" said Sam.

"Okay," said Grandpa. "Let's move the rock into the grass."

"Be careful," said Polly as Grandpa bent his knees and picked up the rock.

"Ooof," said Grandpa as he straightened. He walked a few steps and dropped the rock, just missing his toes.

"There we go," he said.

"Thanks," Polly managed to say as Grandpa went into the house. He had dropped the Earth Child! Polly hoped it wasn't hurt.

She felt all over the rock carefully. It seemed fine. At least it didn't have bones to break.

"Ready?" Sam called. He was standing at the pump.

"Just a second!" Polly called back. She picked up the green hose. "Ready!"

Sam pulled up on the pump's lever. He loved how old it was. It made him feel like a pioneer.

Polly watched as the hose started twitching. It reminded her of the tree roots. Then water came out of the hose in little spurts, like coughs, before turning into a steady stream.

Polly looked at the rock. "This may be a little cold," she told it. She knew from the few drops that had hit her hand that the water was *very* cold. *This must be how doctors feel when they give you a shot,* Polly thought. "It will be over in a minute, I promise."

Sam came running over as Polly turned the stream of water on the rock. He had found some rags by the pump. Together, they carefully washed all the dirt off the rock. Then they turned it over and washed its bottom. After that, they managed to lift it back onto the porch, getting only a little damp in the process.

"Brrr," said Sam. The air was much cooler at night than it was during the day.

"We need to dry it," said Polly.

"I'll get a towel," said Sam. He ran into the house, the screen door slamming behind him.

Polly patted the rock while she waited for him to return.

"You'll be dry very soon," she said. "And I hope I am, too."

Sam burst back out, holding up a light blue towel in triumph.

"Here!" he said, dropping it on the rock.

He and Polly rubbed the rock dry. Then they carefully rolled it over and dried its bottom. The towel was brown by the time they finished.

"Uh-oh," said Sam.

"What are you two doing?" Grandma asked, opening the door.

"We're drying the rock," Polly said. "You

wouldn't want me to not dry it after a bath."

"No," said Grandma, "but I wish you'd asked for an old towel at least." She shook her head. "That one will never be the same again."

Audrey peeked out from behind her. "I would have asked, Grandma," she said.

Grandma stepped onto the porch and held open the door. "Well, you might as well bring it in now that it is clean and dry and my towel is muddy and wet."

Sam handed her the towel before he and Polly bent to lift the rock. They'd just managed to pick it up when—

"I'll help!" said Audrey. She rushed over and squeezed between Sam and Polly. Sam tripped over Audrey. They all wobbled up the low steps toward the door. The rock banged into the doorframe.

"CAREFUL," said Grandma.

"Please don't help," Polly said to Audrey through gritted teeth.

"But I want to," said Audrey.

"Audrey," said Grandma, "why don't you come over here with me?"

Audrey moved out of the way sulkily.

Sam and Polly stumbled into the house with the rock.

"There," said Grandma. "Put it at the foot of the stairs."

"Grandma," said Polly, "we can't take our eyes off it."

"Yeah," said Sam, "or something terrible will happen to it." Sam wasn't sure that was true, but it seemed very possible. Why else would someone turn their child into a rock?

Sam and Polly shuffled past the stairs, down the hall, and through the bathroom to the dining room.

There, they put the rock down carefully on one of the dining room chairs. Grandma and Audrey had followed them in. Grandma shook her head, but she didn't say anything. Sam thought he could see a little smile on her face.

"I thought you could eat in the kitchen

since we already finished dinner," said Grandma, "but this will be fine. Come in and get your bowls."

Polly and Sam both headed into the kitchen with her. They were starving.

Grandma looked at their eager faces.

"Shouldn't one of you stay with your charge?" she asked. "I wouldn't leave a baby alone."

"OH!" said Polly.

"I'll go!" said Audrey.

"You don't count," said Polly.

Audrey's face fell.

"That's not very nice," said Grandma.

"I don't mean it that way," said Polly. "It's just…this is something Sam and I have to do." She looked at Sam pleadingly.

"It's true," said Sam.

Suddenly, there was a loud THUMP. "Yow!" Grandpa hollered from the dining room.

They all rushed in to see what had happened.

Grandpa was leaning against the wall,

holding his foot. His reading glasses hung from one ear. He was looking with astonishment at something on the floor. Everyone else looked at the floor. There was the rock.

"What did you do?" gasped Polly, kneeling beside the rock. Sam dropped to his knees, too. Audrey squeezed between them as they ran their hands over the rock.

"I just wanted to look at it," Grandpa said, his white eyebrows raised high. "And it...it jumped down."

Everyone turned to stare at him.

"Well, maybe not *jumped*," said Grandpa. "Perhaps it just wasn't on the chair very well."

"Okay, everybody," said Grandma. "There's nothing we can do about it now. Leave the rock where it is. I'll get Sam and Polly's dinner." She nodded to Grandpa. "You need to sit down."

Grandpa hobbled sheepishly to a chair.

Audrey followed Grandma into the kitchen. Polly and Sam looked at each other over the rock. Polly tried to make a face that meant, *This is going to be harder than I thought.*

"Are you going to be sick?" Sam asked.

Polly glared at him. "No—"

"Come on, kids," said Grandma. She put a pair of big bowls full of stew on the table. Audrey put down a plate of bread that Grandpa had baked earlier in the day.

Sam and Polly sat down. Grandpa kept shaking his head. Grandma handed them napkins and spoons and knives. Audrey brought them glasses of water with no ice.

"And where is the rock going to sleep tonight?" Grandma asked as they began eating.

"It can stay in our room," said Polly.

"With you and Audrey?" Grandma asked.

"With me and…Audrey?" asked Polly.

"Yes, you two are going to share a room," said Grandma.

Sam could see that Polly was not happy about this. He didn't blame her. Audrey would probably chirp on and on about all the helpful things she'd ever done. Sam tried to think of something.

"But I might be lonely," he said loudly. It

was a babyish thing to say, but he wanted to help Polly.

"Then perhaps the rock should stay with you, to keep you company," said Grandma.

Sam let out a sigh and shrugged his shoulders at Polly.

Polly shrugged back. She knew he had tried.

"How does that sound?" Grandma asked.

Polly and Sam both smiled and nodded. Their mouths were too full to say anything.

CHAPTER FOUR

Runaway Rock

*S*am opened his eyes. It felt early. The room was faintly lit, and chilly air was blowing in through the open window. Sam snuggled under his blanket, ready to fall back to sleep for just a few more minutes.

A branch tapped against his window. Sam squeezed his eyes shut tight and ignored it. But the branch didn't stop its tapping. It seemed to Sam that it got even louder.

He was about to bury his head under his pillow when suddenly he shot upright. The rock! He'd forgotten all about it. He looked down at the floor beside his bed, where he and Polly had put the rock the night before.

But it wasn't there. Polly would kill him! She had told him very clearly that he had to be careful. That he had to take care of the rock by himself. He knew he should have put it in bed with him.

Sam was about to run into Polly's room when he remembered Audrey. It wouldn't be good to wake her up, too. He decided to check outside first. Maybe he had dreamed that Grandma had let them bring it in.

Sam crept downstairs in his pajamas. The narrow wooden stairs creaked. The farmhouse was over a hundred years old and sounded like it. Sam tiptoed past his grandparents' bedroom at the bottom of the stairs to get to the front door.

Sam carefully opened the door and pushed open the screen door. He shivered for a moment in the cool air. Then he stepped out onto the porch and pulled the front door closed. Slowly and quietly, he let the screen door shut.

The rock wasn't on the porch.

Sam gazed around the yard.

There it was.

The lumpy rock sat a few feet away in the dew-laden grass. Sam stared at it. It was dug into the earth again, not as deep as it had been the day before, but at least several inches.

Sam couldn't wait for Polly to wake up. He *had* to get her. This rock wasn't acting like a baby that needed to be taken care of. It was acting like a child that wanted to run away!

Sam turned and yanked open the screen door. He pushed the front door open and remembered just in time to catch the screen door so that it wouldn't slam. Quietly, he hurried up the stairs.

Sam went past his room and peeked into the front bedroom. In one bed, Polly was lying on her side. Half of her dark hair was fanned out on the pillow, the other half wrapped over her face so that it looked as if her whole head was made of hair. Sam had to keep from laughing at the sight.

Audrey was asleep in the other bed. Her thumb was in her mouth. Sam did not want her to wake up and start helping. He would have to be very careful.

He crouched down and crept to the side of Polly's bed and poked her shoulder. She twitched but didn't wake up.

"Pol," he whispered into her ear. He knew she hated that. "The rock's outside. I think—"

She swatted at him.

Sam figured she was awake.

"Shhh," he said quietly. "Audrey."

Polly brushed her hair aside and opened her eyes.

Meet me outside, she mouthed.

Sam nodded. He crept back out of the room. Once he was on the landing, he let out his breath. He hadn't even known he was holding it.

Sam was about to creep downstairs again when he thought about what Polly had said.

She had said "outside." But did "outside" mean outside the room? Or did it mean *outdoors* outside?

Sam was frozen in indecision when Polly tiptoed into the hall with a handful of clothes and the folded parchment. She turned to pull the bedroom door closed. Just as it clicked shut, a little voice said, "I'll help."

Polly and Sam groaned. Polly jerked her head in the direction of Sam's room. They tiptoed in.

"We're just going to pretend we didn't hear that," said Polly, pulling her underwear and jeans on beneath her nightgown. "Come on, Sam, get dressed."

"But, Pol—"

"When we get outside," hissed Polly.

Sam found his jeans from the day before under his bed as Polly pulled a sweater on.

"I'm going," she said, jerking her head in the direction of the stairs.

Sam nodded as he yanked his jeans up over his pajamas.

"Sam," Polly whispered, "take your pajamas off *before* you put your clothes on." Then she slipped out of the room, carrying her hiking boots.

Sam left his pajamas on and found a flannel shirt in his suitcase. He didn't think the Earth Child would care if he had pajamas on under his clothes or not. As he went down the stairs, sneakers in hand, a dark, curly head poked out of the girls' room.

"I'm coming," said Audrey. "I'm helping."

"You can't," said Sam.

"I'm dressed," said Audrey.

"It doesn't matter," said Sam. "You can't come. You're too little."

Audrey's lower lip stuck out and her eyes narrowed. "I'm telling on you," she said slowly.

Sam sighed.

"Fine. Come," he said in an angry whisper. "But don't blame me if Polly's mad at you."

Audrey put her thumb in her mouth and smiled around it.

Sam went down the stairs, shaking his

head. Audrey tiptoed in his wake.

When they came out the door, Polly looked up from where she was kneeling by the rock.

"What's *she* doing here?" asked Polly.

"I'm helping," said Audrey.

"She blackmailed me," said Sam.

"What are you talking about?" said Polly.

"She said she'd tell if we didn't let her help," said Sam.

"Of course she would," snarled Polly.

Audrey gave her a shy smile. "I want to help."

Polly rolled her eyes. "Fine," she said. "The first thing you can do is to go write Grandma and Grandpa a note that says we've gone on a walk around the farm and that we'll be back in time for lunch. Can you do that?"

Audrey nodded her head vigorously. Then she trotted into the house, happy to be on a mission.

As soon as the door closed behind her, Polly turned to Sam and said, "We've got to hide!" She put her hand on the rock. "We'll be back as soon as she's gone," she told it.

Sam and Polly ran around the corner of the house and pushed their way behind a clump of box bushes. It wasn't very comfortable, but it was a good hiding place.

"Do you think this will work?" Sam whispered.

"I don't know," Polly whispered back. "But she'll drive us nuts if she follows us around all day long."

"But if she can't find us, then maybe she'll say we weren't including her," said Sam. "Then we'll get in trouble."

"*I'll* get in trouble," said Polly. "Because I'm the oldest. They'll say I know better."

"I know better, too," said Sam.

"What are you saying? That we should let her come with us?" Polly asked.

"Well…" said Sam. "It's just that she *is* a little tattletale."

"A *big* tattletale." Polly sighed. "Mom and

Dad did say to be on our best behavior."

Just then, they heard Audrey. "Polleeee, how do you spell—" Then they heard the door closing and a little gasp, which must have been Audrey realizing that they weren't there.

"You're right," Polly whispered to Sam. "Let's keep being good." Sometimes Polly wished that being good was not so hard.

They pushed their way out of the box-bushes and went around the corner of the house.

Audrey was standing in the yard with her hands cupped around her mouth, calling to them. At that moment, their grandmother came out of the house in her bathrobe. She did not look happy.

"What are you doing, Audrey?" she said.

Audrey turned and caught sight of Sam and Polly. "There you are!" she said to them.

Grandma turned to look at them, too. She raised one eyebrow, just like their mother did.

"We were playing," said Polly.

"Hide-and-seek," added Sam helpfully.

"That's very nice," said Grandma. "In the future you may want to play a quieter game in the morning. And make sure that Audrey knows all the rules."

Polly and Sam weren't sure what Grandma meant. Either she thought Audrey needed to know that you couldn't call for the people you were looking for or she knew they'd been hiding on purpose.

"Yes, ma'am," they said in unison, an answer that covered all bases.

"I see you've already brought your rock outside," Grandma said.

"Kind of," Sam said under his breath.

"I'm going to make scrambled eggs for breakfast," Grandma went on. "Can you kids run to the chicken coop and see if the hens laid any eggs this morning?"

"Sure," said Polly.

"I'll help," said Audrey.

"Watch out for the rooster," said Grandma. "He can be a little mean sometimes."

"He's a bad rooster," said Audrey.

Sam and Audrey turned to go.

"Wait," said Polly. "We have to take the rock with us."

Grandma smiled. "Of course," she said. Her eyes twinkled. "Too bad we don't have a baby carriage. The wheelbarrow will have to do."

She pointed to the barn. "Over there."

"I'll get it!" said Audrey.

She ran on her short little legs to the barn.

"I think she's going to need some help," said Grandma as they watched Audrey struggle to lift the handles of the big wheelbarrow.

"I'll go," Polly said. "Sam, you watch the rock."

Grandma went inside while Polly and Audrey pushed the wheelbarrow across the yard. Sam looked warily at the rock. Part of him was scared of it, and part of him wanted to help it. He needed to talk to Polly, alone.

Sam waited until Polly sent Audrey into the house to get an old towel to pad the wheelbarrow.

"This rock is really strange," he said.

"Of course it is," said Polly. "It's magic or has a spell on it or something."

"Yeah," said Sam, "but I mean the note says to take care of it, like it's a baby and needs help, but then it keeps trying to get away."

Polly stared at Sam for a moment, then back at the rock. Sam could almost see the thoughts whirling around in her head.

"You're right," she said slowly. Then her eyes narrowed, not unlike Audrey's, and she bit her lip. "Maybe," she began, "maybe it's trying to get away. Or maybe something is *pulling* it away."

Sam shivered. "You mean, like something bad is trying to steal it?"

"Yeah," said Polly.

"Oh," said Sam. He looked around.

The sun had risen above the horizon. The sky was clear except for some high white clouds. The air was warming up, but there was a light, cool breeze. The world was green with tips of gold and orange.

There was nothing sinister about it at all.

Sam let out his breath.

Polly was looking at the ground, thinking some more.

"But how do we know?" she said aloud.

"Huh?" said Sam.

"How do we know if it's trying to get away or if something's trying to steal it?" said Polly.

"I don't know," said Sam. "I guess we had better just keep a good eye on it."

Just then, Audrey bounded out with the towel.

"Should we tell her?" Sam asked Polly.

"What?" Audrey said. "Tell me! What?"

"Nothing," said Polly. She shook her head at Sam. "Not yet."

Audrey's lip went out. "But I want—"

"To help!" said Polly. "Spread the towel in the wheelbarrow while Sam and I pick up the rock."

Audrey's lip tucked back into its proper place and she smiled. "Okay!"

Getting the rock out of the ground took more time than Sam and Polly had expected. It took Grandma's trowel and a lot of digging before they got it loose and could put it into the wheelbarrow.

"Whew," said Polly.

"We could have called again," Sam reminded her.

"I know," she said. "But we should save them for emergencies."

"Save what?" said Audrey.

"Save our breath," said Polly, picking up the wheelbarrow handles, "for getting the eggs."

The three kids trooped past the cars and the vegetable garden to the chicken coop and rabbit hutches. Polly rested the wheelbarrow on the ground beside the hutches. They were empty.

Polly and Sam were sad because it meant the three rabbits that had been there last summer had been eaten by Grandma and Grandpa.

"I miss the rabbits," said Audrey.

"Me too," said Sam.

Polly nodded.

"They're in heaven now," said Audrey.

"Yes," said Polly. "Rabbit heaven. It's filled with lots of happy bunnies and carrots and lettuce."

"And whole fields of grass," said Sam.

Thinking of rabbit heaven made them all feel better. Now they were ready to brave the chicken coop.

The chicken coop was a small shed with chicken wire over its windows. The kids peered through the windows. Inside, the floor was covered with hay and the remains of food scraps. In one corner sat a wooden box, where the chickens sometimes laid eggs.

Altogether, there were four hens and one rooster. One hen was in the box, and the other three were nestled in piles of hay. The rooster was perched on a wooden beam that ran along the top of the coop.

"Here goes," said Polly. She opened the door. Sam came in behind her.

"I don't want to go," said Audrey.

"Watch the rock, then," said Polly. "We'll just be two seconds."

Audrey nodded brightly.

Suddenly, there was a screech and a flutter of wings. The rooster had flown to the floor and was flapping his wings at Sam and Polly.

Polly pulled the door shut behind her.

"SHOO!" she shouted.

The rooster backed up a little.

"Get the eggs," said Polly. "I'll keep the rooster busy."

Polly held the rooster at bay while Sam reached under the hens. Sam loved finding a warm egg, despite the chickens' noise and the fact that the eggs sometimes had chicken poop on them.

Sam found three eggs.

"Got 'em!" he called to Polly.

Suddenly, Audrey screamed.

Sam opened the coop door and Polly dived through. Sam slipped out after her, then shut the door. They heard a THUMP as the rooster threw himself at the door in fury.

"Whew!" said Sam. He held the eggs cradled to his chest.

Polly was catching her breath when Audrey threw her arms around her.

"It's a scary rock!" she said. "I was patting it and it moved! It was coming toward me, but I wouldn't let it."

Audrey was trembling all over.

Sam and Polly looked at each other.

"Go look at the rock," Polly told Sam as she gave Audrey a hug.

Sam looked in the wheelbarrow at the rock. It didn't look any different. He couldn't tell— maybe it had moved just a little bit.

"You did a good job," Polly said to Audrey. "You watched the rock very well."

"I did?" asked Audrey, her tears drying up.

"Yes, you really helped," said Polly. "Now let's go eat!"

She grabbed the handles of the wheelbarrow, and they headed back to the farmhouse.

Sam let Audrey carry an egg.

CHAPTER FIVE

Rock Watching

It was just warm enough to eat breakfast at the picnic table on the back porch. Sam and Polly sat on a bench with the rock between them.

Audrey seemed to have forgotten her fear of the rock. Instead, she chattered on about how it had moved and how she had screamed for help at just the right moment.

Polly didn't try to stop Audrey from talking, because she knew that their grandparents would think that Audrey was only making things up—making things up in a good way, not in a lying way. Polly was right.

"Isn't imagination a wonderful thing?" Grandma asked Grandpa.

"Wonderful," said Grandpa. "And there's something about that funny rock that makes it work overtime."

Sam leaned over to Polly. "Maybe we should ask about the second calling thing," he said softly. "You know. The one about the seed."

Polly nodded. "Um, Grandma," she began, "what's that saying about giant trees growing from little seeds?"

"You mean, 'Giant oaks from tiny acorns grow'?" Grandma asked.

"Yeah," said Polly. "That's it."

"What about it?" asked Grandma.

"Oh," said Polly, "Sam and I were just talking about it, and we couldn't remember it exactly."

"Are there any oak trees around here?"

asked Sam, casually looking down at his eggs.

"A few," said Grandpa.

"And acorns," said Polly. "Where could we get one?"

"I don't know about that," said Grandma. "You usually find them in the spring."

"I've got some," said Grandpa. "I always have a few around on my dresser or in my desk drawers."

"Can we have one?" asked Sam.

"Sure," said Grandpa.

Sam and Polly leaped to their feet.

"After breakfast," said Grandma.

They sat back down. As they did, they felt the rock shift. Sam and Polly each gave a little jump.

"What's wrong?" asked Grandpa. "The rock give you a pinch?"

"Sam must have pushed it," said Polly.

"No, I didn't," said Sam. "You must have nudged it."

"Or it moved on its own," said Grandma, putting homemade jam on a piece of toast.

"It moved again," said Audrey. She began chanting, "The rock moved. The rock moved..."

Sam and Polly looked at each other. It was going to be a very long day.

After breakfast, the kids decided to take a picnic and go on a hike into the woods to a place where there was the foundation of an old cabin. Polly and Audrey put the rock back into the wheelbarrow. Grandma packed them a lunch.

Grandpa found an acorn and gave it to Sam. Sam put the acorn safely in his pocket and went out to the wheelbarrow.

"You forgot the picnic stuff," said Polly.

"I thought you'd gotten it," said Sam.

Polly sighed. "I have to do everything around here," she said.

"That's not true! I got the acorn!" called Sam as Polly went inside.

Grandma gave Polly the picnic, packed in a grocery bag.

"Stay on the path," said Grandma. "We

don't want you getting lost."

"We won't," said Polly.

"And take good care of Audrey," said Grandma.

"I will," said Polly.

Outside, Audrey was tucking the towel around the rock in the wheelbarrow.

"Now she *wants* it to move," Sam said. "She wants it to be her baby."

"Of course," said Polly. She handed Sam the picnic bag and picked up the handles of the wheelbarrow. "Let's go."

Polly pushed the wheelbarrow onto the gravel road. They walked up past the chicken coop, then went past the greenhouse that always needed cleaning and the windmill that didn't work. Finally, they went around the old soybean field and walked along the edge of the woods.

Polly was not having a good time pushing the wheelbarrow. The whole thing wobbled. The wheel kept getting stuck in ruts. And once it nearly tipped over.

Audrey skipped ahead, and Sam wandered behind. No one was helping Polly as she struggled—no one was even keeping her company! Polly got grouchier and grouchier each time the wheelbarrow ran into a hole.

Finally, she stopped.

Sam ran into her.

"I need some help," Polly said. "You guys aren't paying any attention. I'm hauling the rock all by myself. I wish we could just leave it right here!"

Audrey looked back at them and started sucking her thumb.

"We can't leave it," said Sam. "What about the magic?"

"I don't care about the magic," snapped Polly. "This is too much work. We have to take it wherever we go. And it's not even like it's a little kid you can play games with. It's a rock! Besides, you're supposed to get paid to baby-sit. And now I know why."

Sam was silent for a moment. Audrey had walked back to them during Polly's tirade, and the only sound now was a thumb-sucking slurping.

"Stop sucking your thumb, Audrey," said Polly. "It's gross."

Audrey took her thumb out of her mouth. "I don't care," she said. "You're mean. I'm telling."

"Fine," said Polly. "Tell."

"I'll push the wheelbarrow," said Sam, changing the subject.

"Fine," said Polly.

They kept walking. Polly's anger slowly fell away. It was a relief not to be pushing the wheelbarrow. She was careful to stay near Sam, because she hadn't liked being left alone herself.

"I never realized how hard it is," Polly said.

"What?" asked Sam.

"Taking care of something," she answered. "Having to watch it. All the time."

"At least we don't have to feed it or change its diapers," said Sam. "That's what real baby-sitters do."

"Thank goodness for that," said Polly. "Hey, here it is!"

They had reached the path into the woods. A hush fell.

The three kids stopped and peered into the shadows beneath the trees.

All of a sudden, neither Polly nor Sam wanted to go down the path. They looked at each other nervously. In the silence, Polly's hand drifted over to touch the rock. It felt warm.

The moment of quiet seemed to go on and on, as if the woods were waiting for them to make a choice: to enter or not.

Then Audrey gave a happy shout and skipped onto the path.

CHAPTER SIX

Into the Woods

"Come on!" Audrey called as a breeze rustled in the trees.

The silence was broken. Beneath the trees lay dappled sunlight, not dark shadows. Audrey's curly head bobbed up and down and her scarf flew after her as she skipped along the path.

As quickly as the ominous feeling had come, it went. Polly and Sam smiled sheepishly at each other.

"For a moment…" began Sam.

"Yeah. Me too," said Polly.

She and Sam looked down the path. Audrey had stopped and was waving at them.

"I wonder why she didn't feel it," Sam said.

"She's too little," said Polly.

"Maybe," said Sam. He picked up the handles of the wheelbarrow. "It's not trying to get away anymore."

"The rock?" said Polly.

"Yeah," said Sam.

"Maybe it's just napping," said Polly.

"I hope it stays napping all morning," said Sam.

"And then all afternoon, too," said Polly. "Don't you think its mother will come get it soon?"

"Or its father," said Sam.

Polly looked down the path again. Audrey was disappearing through the trees.

"Hey!" called Polly. "Audrey, don't go any farther! Come on, Sam. We're really babysitting the two of them."

Polly trotted under the trees. Sam looked up at the blue sky before pushing the wheelbarrow onto the leafy path. He was happy to know that he had the acorn. If anything happened, at least they could get help.

The light coming through the leaves was green and gold. The trees stood tall. The wheelbarrow bumped along the path, rolling over twigs and dry leaves. The air was the tiniest bit chilly. Sam could see Audrey's red scarf through the trees. Polly whistled in front of him, her dark braid swinging.

Sam smiled. Even the weight of the rock in the wheelbarrow didn't bother him.

The path went down a hill. The trees here all leaned back as if they didn't want to slide to the bottom. Sam had to hold tight to the wheelbarrow so that it wouldn't get away from him.

Audrey's voice came from up ahead. "I found it! I found the cabin!"

"You okay, Sam?" Polly asked, turning around.

Sam concentrated on keeping the wheelbarrow steady and nodded.

"I'm going on, all right?" said Polly.

"Uh-huh," said Sam. He couldn't look up.

He heard Polly run down the path after Audrey, the girls' voices twisting together somewhere at the foot of the hill.

The wheelbarrow began pulling Sam forward, the wheel bouncing along. It rolled faster and faster. Sam gave up trying to hold it back. Instead, he just tried to keep up with it.

He stumbled over sticks and roots, but he kept going. He tried to look up and caught a blur of light and leaves.

"Watch out below!" he called.

Polly and Audrey glanced up from where they were standing in the center of a sunken square. The square was lined with stones, and a tumble-down stone chimney rose on one side.

Sam was hurtling straight down the hill toward them, the wheelbarrow in front of him. They could see the rock bouncing in the wheelbarrow.

"Sam!" screamed Audrey.

"Let go!" yelled Polly.

But Sam's hands were frozen to the wheelbarrow handles as it hurtled into the old foundation. The wheelbarrow hit the stone border. But it didn't stop.

It leaped over it and dived toward the ground in front of Polly and Audrey. There was a sucking sound as the wheelbarrow slid into the earth, pulling Sam behind it.

"Let go!" Polly shouted again as Sam's arms sank into the earth.

"I can't!" Sam shouted.

The dirt was cold and wet on his hands, and it pressed against his arms. Sam wondered if he could get to the acorn, but he couldn't possibly reach his pocket. *This* was a real emergency. He took a deep breath and held it as his head went under.

Polly could hardly believe what she was seeing as Sam's blond head sank into the dirt. It was horrible!

Audrey was shrieking, and Polly wanted to

do the same. Instead, she grabbed Sam's feet, which now were the only part of him showing.

"Get out, Audrey," Polly shouted. "Run!"

Audrey didn't move. She just watched with wide eyes.

Polly braced her feet as the dirt in the old foundation began to move in a circle, like a giant whirlpool.

The last thing Polly saw was Audrey's open mouth as the dirt swept Audrey's feet out from under her. Then Polly felt a small hand catch her ankle, and she, too, sank into the earth.

CHAPTER SEVEN

Underground

Sam was lying on something soft. Maybe he'd dreamed about getting sucked under the earth. Maybe he was in bed. He pressed his cheek into the softness. It was fuzzy. He didn't have fuzzy sheets!

Sam opened his eyes. Then he shut them. There was no difference. He opened them again. Then he reached up with his hand to see if his eyes were really open.

"Ouch!" His eyes were definitely open. And

now one of them hurt from having had a finger stuck in it. Sam realized he was in the dark. He also realized he must be underground. His heart started to thud. What if he was buried in a coffin, like in an old horror movie he'd seen once?

Slowly, Sam sat up, waiting for his head to bang against dirt or wood or even the funny fuzziness that was underneath him. His head didn't hit anything. He stretched his arms out in front of him. Nothing was there.

Sam breathed a small sigh of relief. At least he wasn't in a coffin. But his ankles hurt a little. He reached down to rub them and remembered Polly grabbing him. Maybe she was here, too. That would be great!

"Polly!" he called.

He heard coughing and moving.

"Sam," said Polly.

She sounded as if she was right next to him. He felt around and touched something damp and woolly. It was Polly's sweater.

Polly grabbed his hand.

"Sam," she said, her voice clearer. "We're underground somewhere."

"I figured," said Sam.

"Oh, no!" said Polly. "Where's Audrey? Where's the rock?"

"Audrey!" called Sam.

"I'm here," came a little voice.

Sam and Polly groped around until they found Audrey. They hugged each other in a muddle, like newborn puppies. It was all Polly could do not to whimper.

"The rock," she said.

Audrey wouldn't let go of Polly's right hand, so she had to feel around with her left. She could hear Sam moving beside her.

"Got it," he said. "Or at least I have the wheelbarrow."

There was a pause. Then there was a little sound—a little live, gurgling sound.

"What is that?" said Polly.

"Uh, um…I think there's something else in the wheelbarrow," said Sam.

"What?" said Polly.

"I think it's a baby," said Sam.

"WHAT?" said Polly again.

"A baby," said Sam. "You know, b-a-b-y."

The gurgling turned to a little giggle. In the darkness, the giggle seemed very creepy to Sam.

"Sam," said Polly. "You have the acorn."

"Right!" said Sam. He reached into his pocket. It was filled with dirt. Sam turned his pocket inside out.

"What are you doing now?" asked Polly.

"I, um, I think I just dropped the acorn," said Sam. "It was by accident."

"I want to see the baby!" Audrey suddenly said.

"Well, none of us can see anything right now," said Polly. "We have to find the acorn, Sam."

"But I want—" began Audrey.

"You go talk to the baby while Sam and I find the acorn, then," said Polly.

She pushed Audrey in the direction of Sam's voice. Audrey gave a little squeal. Then Sam said, "I've got you."

Polly crawled toward Sam's voice, too.

"Yow!" she said. Her knee had landed on something hard. She reached down and felt something small and round. She was about to throw it away when she realized what it was.

"I got it," she said.

"The acorn?" asked Sam.

"Yes!" said Polly. "I'm going to call."

"Acorn!" came a tiny, sweet voice.

"Who's that?" Sam and Polly both said.

"It's the baby!" said Audrey.

"Babies can't talk," said Polly. She lifted the acorn to her mouth. "Hello?" There was no answer. "Hello!" she called a little louder. "We need help in here! This is an emergency!"

A whispery voice echoed around them. "Emergency lights on," it said.

The walls began to glow with a green light. They saw they were in a small, square cave with a mossy floor. Sam saw Polly kneeling on the floor, holding the acorn. Audrey was bent over the wheelbarrow. Peeking out of it was a small brown head with round brown eyes.

"Yay!" said Audrey.

"Yay!" said the baby.

"It's not a *baby* baby," Polly said. "It's like a big baby."

"Well, it was a baby baby when *I* felt it," said Sam. "Maybe it's grown up a bit."

"That's silly," Polly scoffed. "A real baby couldn't grow that fast."

"Yeah," said Sam, "but a rock that turns into a baby isn't very real, either. This is a magic baby. It could grow super-fast."

"Super-fast!" chortled the toddler.

"I think it *is* getting bigger!" said Audrey. "Its head looks bigger."

"Well, there's nothing I can do about that," said Polly. "At least we have light. I guess that's a help. Now we better try to get out of here. Grandma is not going to be happy about this. *I'm* not very happy about it."

Sam was about to agree when he realized he wasn't sure how he felt about it. Since he hadn't died when the ground ate him, he was feeling a lot better about things. In fact, it was even starting to feel like an adventure!

Polly looked around for a way out. Tree roots curled along the ceiling and walls. Strange mushrooms grew in clumps in the moss on the floor and on the walls. She saw some worms wiggling around, but she didn't want to look too closely at them.

"It's so pretty!" said Audrey.

Polly stared at her.

"The roots make pretty shapes," said Audrey.

"They do," said Sam. "It's neat."

Polly looked around again. Maybe she was getting used to the cave, because it didn't seem as ominous as it had a moment before.

"Yeah," said Polly. "I guess it is kind of nice."

"Without roots there would be no trees," Sam said thoughtfully. "They're like veins or something." He stopped. "That makes sense. If the ground, the ground that's up there"—Sam pointed up—"is the skin, then this is like the insides."

"Ugh," said Polly. "That's gross."

"It's like being inside the world's body," Sam continued in a hushed voice.

"Yeah, well, we need to find a way out of the body and back to the skin," said Polly.

"That way," said Sam.

He pointed to one corner of the cave. There, partly hidden by roots and partly made of them, was an archway.

"I'll push the wheelbarrow," said Polly.

Audrey wrapped the towel around the baby. The wheelbarrow was filled with dirt, which the baby seemed to like.

Sam walked ahead of them to the arch.

"It looks like a tunnel," he said.

Polly pushed the wheelbarrow over. It was a tunnel, a very long one. It was filled with the same greenish light and tangled roots as the square cave. It was wide enough for two of them to walk side by side.

Polly and Sam each took a deep breath. Audrey was watching them and did the same. As they let their breaths out, they stepped through the arch into the tunnel.

Sam walked next to Polly. Audrey stayed beside the wheelbarrow and talked to the baby.

"You're good at that, Audrey," said Sam.

"Yeah," said Polly, "and that's good for us. We have to figure out what the third thing is that we can use to call for help. Although if a bit of light counts as help in an emergency, I'm not sure it will do any good."

"It has to help at least a little," said Sam.

Polly sighed. "Get the parchment out of my pocket. Let's see exactly what it says."

Sam pulled the parchment out of Polly's pocket. Folded, it looked like a little mushroom. Sam unfolded it and held it out. Polly didn't stop walking, but she slowed down to look at it.

"Something 'ella of the mouse,'" she said. "All I can think of is Cinderella."

"It can't be that," said Sam.

"Look!" said Audrey. "Look at the baby!"

The baby was kneeling in the wheelbarrow, as if she was ready to stand. She was about two feet tall. Her hair was long and the bright yellow-green of new leaves. It curled like the fiddlehead of a fern. Her fingernails and toe-nails were also bright green.

"I want to walk," she said clearly.

Polly stopped short. It was occurring to her that this baby was a little person—a cheery baby version of the punk-rock kids who dyed their hair wild colors and hung out at the mall.

"What's your name?" Polly asked the child.

"Don't know," she answered.

"We have to call her something," said Polly.

"How about Earth?" said Sam. "'Cause she's an Earth Child."

"Earth," said the child.

Audrey stood back as Polly lifted Earth out of the wheelbarrow. The towel that had been wrapped around her had become a little grassy dress that hung to her fat knees when she was standing.

"I'll help," said Audrey. She held her hand out to Earth.

Polly picked up the handles of the wheelbarrow, and they started walking again. Without Earth, the wheelbarrow was much lighter, but they still had to go slowly. Earth didn't walk very fast, although she was growing bigger with every step.

For a while, Sam watched her with fascination. It was like something that happened on a television show about outer space or the future. Sometimes Earth grew a lot at once, then minutes would go by and she'd stay the same.

Finally, Sam got tired of it and began looking down the tunnel.

Polly was trying to figure out what she could possibly do to get them home when Sam tapped her shoulder.

"Do you hear that?" he asked.

Polly came out of her jumble of thoughts. There was a familiar, steady rushing sound. As they walked on, it grew a little louder.

Ahead, there was a bright light.

"The end of the tunnel!" said Sam.

Polly could see movement through the entrance, but in the greenness it was hard to make out what it was. And roots blocked the way.

At that moment, a worm fell on her shoulder.

Polly screamed and shook it off.

"It won't hurt you," said Sam.

"I know," said Polly, embarrassed by her scream. "It startled me."

Audrey and Earth, who looked nearly the same age now, squatted down and looked at the worm. Earth patted it. Then Audrey picked it up and moved it to the side of the tunnel, where it burrowed into the dirt.

"Come on," Polly said gruffly. Now she was even more embarrassed.

They walked out of the tunnel into a huge underground room. The ceiling opened up until it was as big as the sky, and smooth pebbles rolled under their feet. A river rushed by in front of them, the sound of its current muffled. Mist hung like a thick blanket over the water, making it impossible to see to the other side.

CHAPTER EIGHT

New Names

"Styx," said Earth, pointing at the mist-covered water.

"That's not sticks," said Polly. "It's a river."

"Yes," said Earth, who now looked older than Sam. "The River Styx, that's its name."

Sam frowned. He thought it sounded vaguely familiar.

"How do you spell it?" Polly asked.

"S-t-y-x," Earth spelled out. "It is the river of the Underworld."

"This is definitely the Underworld," said Sam.

"We must cross the river," said Earth.

"Why?" said Polly. Everything was muffled—not just the sound of the river, but her thoughts, too.

"It is the only way to get out," said Earth.

"How do you know?" asked Polly.

"I just do," Earth said with a toss of her green hair. "Sometimes the only way to get out of something is to go deeper into it."

"Huh?" said Sam. "I don't get it."

Earth nodded, and her forehead wrinkled. "I don't get it, either. I just know that it's true," she said. "There are things that I understand but don't know why. There is some part of me I can't find."

"I'll help you find it!" offered Audrey.

Earth smiled down at her.

"I bet that when you're older, you'll find it," said Polly. "That's what people always tell me. Of course, you're growing pretty fast, so maybe it'll be soon."

"Maybe," said Earth. She turned to the river.

Polly thought she could see the brown-and-green girl growing taller out of the corner of her eye. It was like watching a flower growing and blossoming at high speed, like they did on nature shows.

The mist hung unmoving over the gray-green water. Then out of it came a shadow gliding along the surface of the river. As it drew closer, the shadow became more solid, until it was a boat with a tall figure at one end. The figure used a pole to push the boat forward. The boat slid across the swift current, making no mark on the gray-green water.

Sam gulped. "I guess the water isn't that deep, huh?"

"It is," said Earth. "He's just got a very long pole."

"I'm not so sure about this," said Polly.

"Me neither," said Sam.

"Should we go back?" Polly said, looking toward the entrance to the tunnel.

"It's too late now," said Earth.

And it seemed to be, as Sam and Polly found their feet moving all by themselves and taking them toward the river.

"Help!" said Sam.

"It's got me, too," said Polly.

Earth and Audrey were holding hands and laughing.

Earth turned back, now a teenager with an open smile. "Go with the flow," she said. "Don't resist."

"Easy for her to say," muttered Polly.

Sam shut his eyes and let his feet lead him. He figured the magic wouldn't let him fall. It was a strange feeling, as if he were already caught in the current of the water and it was pulling him along.

Polly let herself go, too. But she watched every step of the way. And she watched the shadowy boat, as well, as it neared the shore. The boat's captain was a long, thin man the same color as the water.

Polly was about to protest when the boat's

prow hit the rocks and the pulling stopped. Sam nearly fell over. He opened his eyes, a little cross that the pull had stopped so abruptly, just when he'd gotten used to it.

The boatman looked up. Even the whites of his eyes were gray-green.

When he saw Earth, his face broke into a gray smile. Earth's eyes widened, and Polly could almost see memory rushing into them.

"Charon!" said Earth.

"Young Persephone," said the boatman in a stately manner. "You are very late this year. Step in."

"I am *Persephone!*" said Earth quietly. "Yes."

At the sound of what seemed to be Earth's real name, Polly's mind started working. Sam could see she wasn't paying any attention to what was happening. The name sounded familiar to him, too, but the situation was too interesting to miss.

"I must bring my friends," said Persephone.

Charon the boatman peered around her, his body twisting like a long reed.

"I don't know," he said doubtfully. "I don't have the right feeling about them."

"They can't go any other way," said Persephone. "I need help to get them back to where they belong."

"What about payment?" Charon asked.

"This is not the time to get stingy," said Persephone.

"But I haven't had customers in a long time," the boatman protested. "This way is not often traveled these days."

Persephone sighed. "I don't have the usual," she said.

"I'll take what you can give," the boatman said.

Persephone closed her eyes and whistled softly. At their feet, three shoots of green poked out from between the rocks. They grew leaves and blossomed into white daisies.

Audrey stooped, as if to pick them.

"Don't!" cried the boatman.

Audrey recoiled quickly.

"I like them growing," explained the boatman with a small, pleased smile.

Audrey smiled back at him. "Me too," she said.

"Climb in," he said.

The boat wobbled as they stepped into it: first the three kids, then Persephone. They squeezed past the boatman. There were two rows of seats. Sam, Audrey, and Polly took the ones at the back.

Sam glanced over at Polly, who in turn was watching Persephone as she sat in the middle seat, nearest Charon. Persephone looked as if her mind were far away, working out some important problem.

"Can I help?" Audrey asked the boatman as he pushed off the shore.

"Oh, no!" said Sam. "We left Grandpa's wheelbarrow!"

CHAPTER NINE

Land of the Dead

The mist enveloped the small boat. Sam watched as the shore—and the wheelbarrow—disappeared.

"Don't worry," said Persephone, looking back and mistaking his expression. "There is another side."

Then Persephone leaned toward the boatman and began talking to him in a low voice.

"What are we going to tell Grandpa?" Sam said.

"I think we have a bigger problem than that," said Polly. "We're mixed up in that crazy family again."

"What crazy family?" asked Sam.

"The Greek gods, or whatever they are," Polly whispered. "I think I've figured out what's going on. There's this story that a long time ago Persephone was kidnapped by the God of the Underworld. Persephone's mother is the Goddess of the Earth, and she was so sad about her daughter that she made fall and winter happen. And then Persephone came back, and it was spring again."

"But we have fall and winter every year," said Sam.

"Yeah," said Polly. "That's because Persephone ate something down here, so every year she has to come back for six months. Her mother still isn't very happy about it."

"Are you talking about me?" Persephone asked. She turned to them, a smile playing on her lips. "It sounds like you know my story."

"It's true?" said Sam.

"Well, stories don't stay the same when they are told a lot," said Persephone. "And it all happened so long ago. Time changes almost everything. But the basic story is true enough. I actually like coming here for half the year. The only problem is that my mother is forever trying to keep me home. She needs to get a life."

"Did your mother turn you into a rock?" asked Sam.

"Yes," said Persephone.

"But doesn't she think she's trying to save you?" asked Polly.

"Yes," said Persephone, "but...well, because I don't want to hurt her feelings, I've never told her that I *like* to be down here."

"Then it is a bit your fault," said Sam.

"Yes," sighed Persephone. "It is."

"But why were you a rock?" asked Polly. "Why were you a baby? Why did we have to take care of you?"

"I think she was trying to hide me," said Persephone.

"Oh," said Sam.

Suddenly, the boat hit the shore with a bump.

The air shimmered with hurrying gray shadows. It was a world as gray-green as the river, with the same feeling of openness above. Sam tried to see things more clearly, but it just made his eyes water.

A terrifying howl split the air.

A giant dog leaped through the shadows, running toward the boat. The three kids screamed as it jumped into the river beside them. Water and dog drool flew everywhere. And there was a lot of it, because this dog had three heads.

Polly and Sam and Audrey scrambled to get away from dog spit and teeth and growling. When they all were squashed as deep in the rocking boat as they could go without being pressed against Charon, they peeked back. The dog was standing in the water, licking Persephone. She had her arms around his necks and was laughing.

"Down, boy, good boy," she said. "I know you missed me. I missed you, too."

She looked up at the kids. "This is the biggest reason I always want to come down here!" she said. "His name is Cerberus."

"Cool," said Sam. "I wish *I* had a dog."

Audrey was the first to creep forward. "May I pet him?" she asked Persephone shyly.

"Sure," Persephone answered. "And you may call me Per. Now let's get out of this boat."

Gingerly, they climbed onto the shore.

They were greeted by the wet dog, who was standing in a puddle of water and drool. Sam slipped in it, and Polly stepped carefully around it. The boatman shook his head ruefully.

"Always got to mop up after that creature," he said. "It just loves Per."

"Thanks for the ride," said Polly.

"Anytime," said Charon.

"I hope not," whispered Sam as the boat slipped away into the mist.

Persephone stepped forward into the fuzzy, muffled world along a fuzzy gray path. The three kids followed in a daze. The grayness was arranged in shapes and shadows that could have been houses or piles of rocks. Other shapes and shadows moved like animals or people. Sam gave up trying to see them, and Polly tried to ignore them altogether. Audrey talked to Cerberus, who was trotting along beside them.

Some shadows hovered around them as they walked along. Persephone called the shadows by name and talked to them, although the kids couldn't understand what she was saying.

"She must see them more clearly than we do," said Polly.

"I hope so," said Sam. "When do you think we'll go home?"

"Oh!" said Polly. "That's right." She called ahead to Persephone. "Excuse me, but how are we going to get home?"

Persephone stopped and turned. "I'm so sorry. I completely forgot about that! I have so much on my mind. Let's see. It's not easy."

"But you can do magic," said Audrey. "You made the flowers grow."

Persephone's brown forehead wrinkled in thought.

"Maybe you can come with me when I go back up in six months," said Persephone.

"We can't wait that long!" said Polly. "We're not grown-up like you. I need to live with my parents still, not just visit them! And Grandma will be furious if I don't get Audrey back to her."

"Hey, Pol—" Sam began.

"And what about Sam?" Polly carried on. "I'll get in trouble for Sam, too. And then—"

"Polly!" Sam shouted. "I have an answer."

Polly stared at him. "You do?"

"Yeah," Sam said proudly. "The 'ella of the mouse'!"

"The 'ella of the mouse,'" said Polly quietly. "That's it." She dug in her pocket and pulled out the mushroom-shaped folded parchment. She stared at it. "And now I know what the 'ella of the mouse' is!"

"You do?" said Sam.

Polly beamed. "Yup! It's 'ella' for '*umb*rella.'

And the umbrella of a mouse is a mushroom!"

"You're right!" said Sam.

Polly held up the folded parchment. "We were so dumb. There was a clue all along!"

"It looks like a mushroom!" said Audrey. She didn't know what was going on, but she was happy to help.

"It does," said Polly. She turned to Persephone, her cheerfulness restored. "Okay, these were things we could use to call for help when we were watching you. Do you think we can use the last one to help ourselves now?"

Persephone smiled. "I think my mother would agree that you have earned it. All of you."

Polly smiled back at her. "Do you have a mushroom I could borrow?" she asked.

Persephone walked over to a patch of grayness and pulled a mushroom from the ground. It was light brown with green spots. She handed it to Polly.

Polly held it by the stem.

"Hello," she called into the top of the

mushroom. "Our job is done. The baby's grown-up. We didn't let her out of our sight—well, hardly ever. We can't take care of her anymore, she's taking care of herself."

There was no answer.

"Uh, and...and we need some help ourselves now," Polly went on awkwardly. "Do you think you could possibly do anything for us? If it's not too much to ask? I know things didn't work out quite as planned, but..." her voice trailed off.

There was still no answer.

Polly let her hand drop. "Maybe she thinks we did a bad job," she said.

"You didn't do a bad job," said Persephone. "You were great." She squared her shoulders. "Let me see that mushroom," she said.

Polly handed it over.

"Mother," Persephone said into the mushroom. "These kids were incredible. It's not fair for you not to keep your promise to help in an emergency. Do you want to make another mother unhappy?"

They all waited.

Then Persephone whispered, "Look."

Something purple rolled out of the shadows in front of them. It was a small ball of yarn. A strand of it disappeared into the shadows.

"There's your answer," said Persephone. "Thank you," she said into the mushroom. "I'll call you later."

She picked up the ball of yarn and put it into Polly's hands.

"We follow the piece of yarn?" asked Polly.

"Yes," said Persephone. "It's a pretty traditional way to get out of a confusing place."

Then she gave each of them a hug, and Cerberus barked and licked them with each of his three tongues.

"Yuck," said Polly, but very quietly.

Finally, Persephone reached into an invisible pocket and gave each of them a funny-looking seed.

"To remember me by," she said. "Thank you."

"No problem," said Sam.

"One more thing," said Persephone, her dark eyes gazing into theirs. "Don't look back."

Audrey took Polly's hand as they walked. They were careful not to look back, but it was harder than it seemed.

"I hate when people tell you not to do something you probably wouldn't do anyway, and then all you can think about is how you want to do it," complained Polly.

Sam nodded in agreement.

Now they all tried to ignore the flitting shadows and the grayness that pressed up against them.

Polly wound up the yarn as they went along. The farther away from Persephone they got, the darker the air became. The stark quietness gathered around them.

"I think the shadows are ghosts," said Sam.

"I know," said Polly. "Let's not think about it. They're not bad ghosts."

"I'm scared," said Audrey.

"We have to do something," said Polly. "Let's sing!"

They ended up singing Christmas carols, the safest and most comforting songs they could think of. Soon they were singing in pure darkness.

"I guess the emergency lights have failed," said Sam between carols.

"It's okay, though," said Polly brightly. "I have the yarn!"

"I miss Earth," whimpered Audrey.

"Hey," said Sam, "do you see something ahead?"

It was a pinprick of light, like a single star in a night sky.

CHAPTER TEN

Fall

Sam, Polly, and Audrey walked toward the light. It got bigger and bigger, until they could see trees and sky through it.

Then they were squeezing between two giant rocks, breathless. They all looked around.

"Now *this* is beautiful," said Polly.

They had come out at the edge of the woods, near a stream at the bottom of a sloping hill. It was on the side of the Farm opposite where they had been sucked into the ground.

The yarn went up into a tall tree.

Polly tugged on it to see if it would come loose. When it didn't, she put the ball of yarn at the tree's base, between its roots. Audrey and Sam watched.

"Thank you," she said.

Audrey and Sam said, "Thank you," too.

Then they all heard a low humming sound. Over the crest of the hill came Grandpa on the red tractor. He was looking up at the clouds as the tractor bumped along.

"He should be watching where he's going," said Polly.

Just then, they heard a voice shouting over the tractor's hum, "Watch where you're going, Marshall!"

Marshall was Grandpa's name, and the voice was Grandma's. She was riding in the hay cart.

The three kids watched as Grandpa stopped the tractor. He climbed down, and Grandma hopped out of the cart. They held hands and looked up at the sky together.

Audrey couldn't stand it a moment longer.

"Grandpa! Grandma!" she shouted, running toward them.

Polly and Sam waited only a moment before they started running, too. Grandma looked very surprised to see her three grandchildren racing toward them, streaked with dirt.

Grandpa just laughed. "Lost my wheelbarrow, did you?" he boomed as they ran up.

"It's a long story," said Sam.

"And where's the Earth Child?" asked Grandma. She noticed everything.

"Gone back to her mother," said Audrey.

Grandma gave Audrey a squeeze, despite the streaks of dirt. "And where on earth have you been?" she asked.

"We've been *in* the earth!" said Audrey. "It was fun! And look what I got!" She held up one of the funny-looking seeds from Persephone.

Grandma shook her head. "It certainly looks like you've been underground. But I can't imagine where you got a pomegranate seed."

She hugged Sam. "You'll all need a long bath. We thought you were on the other side of the Farm. That's a long hike—you could have gotten lost!"

"I'd never lose Sam or Audrey," Polly said.

"I would hope not," said Grandma, putting an arm around her. "But you know, Polly, I hope they watched out for you, too. I really don't want to lose *you*, either."

Polly had never thought about it that way. She leaned against her grandmother. "Yes," she said, "they looked after me, too."

"Good," said Grandma. Then she gave Sam a funny look. "Sam, are those your pajamas I see under your clothes?"

Later, Sam tried to fall asleep. He felt very tired, but his mind wouldn't stop racing. He felt as if he'd never found out so many interesting new things all at once in his whole life.

He climbed out of bed. The air coming through the window was pleasantly chilly. He picked up the quilt folded at the end of his bed. Then he wrapped it around himself and tiptoed downstairs.

Polly was standing in the yard with her blanket wrapped around her.

"Your daughter's coming back," Sam heard her say when he opened the door. "And she's really okay. She likes it. It's different, you know."

The two big trees in the yard rustled their leaves, whispering sadness and questions as clearly as words.

Polly went on, "And she has a dog. It's big and drooly and has three heads, but she loves it. And she loves you, too, of course. I promise she'll tell you all this herself, but in case you want to get used to the idea—"

Polly stopped when she heard the door close, even though it closed quietly.

"Oh, hi, Sam," she said. "I'm just, you know..."

Sam nodded. "I know," he said. "I think you're doing the right thing."

The leaves waved in agreement.

"It's so weird how things can be different from what they seem," said Polly.

"Yeah," said Sam. "Like we thought we were protecting the rock, the Earth Child— Persephone—from something bad, but really we were fighting the way things work."

"And Audrey being brave and actually saying some things other than 'I'll help,'" said Polly. "Being a person, with ideas and stuff."

Sam laughed. And a littler voice laughed with him.

Audrey stepped out of the house, her white nightgown making her look ghostly.

"But Sam and I *did* help you," she said. "Even though you're the oldest. You didn't have to do it all by yourself."

"No," said Polly. "I didn't. We're all very lucky to have each other."

The trees whispered again, quietly and contentedly.

Polly spread her blanket on the grass under one of the trees.

No one spoke as they sat down on the blanket and pulled Sam's quilt around them for warmth.

They looked up at the stars through the tree branches as leaves began to fall like snowflakes. By the time their eyes closed, they were covered with a quilt of autumn colors.

And the trees sighed as the Earth settled down for its winter sleep.

If you enjoyed

Earth Magic,

check out

the *first* book in

The Magic Elements Quartet,

Water Wishes.

And don't miss the *next* book in

The Magic Elements Quartet

when Polly and Sam find

another message

and another mystery in

Wind Spell.

MALLORY LOEHR lives in Brooklyn, New York, but her grandparents do have a farm outside of Charlottesville, Virginia, which she visits as often as possible (but not often enough). She did get lost in the woods with her younger brother one time; luckily, it was not for too long. Some of her favorite authors growing up were (and still are!) Diana Wynne Jones, Lloyd Alexander, Madeleine L'Engle, and Edward Eager. Ms. Loehr loves to read, write, sew pillows, and see anyone in her family. Fall is her favorite season.

GRADES 1–3

Duz Shedd series
    by Marjorie Weinman Sharmat

Junie B. Jones series by Barbara Park

Magic Tree House series
    by Mary Pope Osborne

Marvin Redpost series by Louis Sachar

Clyde Robert Bulla
The Chalk Box Kid
The Paint Brush Kid
White Bird

Jackie French Koller
Mole and Shrew All Year Through

Jerry Spinelli
Tooter Pepperday
Blue Ribbon Blues: A Tooter Tale

GRADES 2–4

A to Z Mysteries series by Ron Roy

Polly Berrien Berends
The Case of the Elevator Duck

Ann Cameron
Julian, Dream Doctor
Julian, Secret Agent
Julian's Glorious Summer

Adèle Geras
Little Swan

Stephanie Spinner & Jonathan Etra
Aliens for Breakfast
Aliens for Lunch
Aliens for Dinner

Gloria Whelan
Next Spring an Oriole
Silver
Hannah
Night of the Full Moon

GRADES 3–5

Fiction

The Magic Elements Quartet
  by Mallory Loehr
#1: Water Wishes
#2: Earth Magic

Mary Pope Osborne
#1: Spider Kane and the Mystery
  Under the May-Apple
#2: Spider Kane and the Mystery
  at Jumbo Nightcrawler's

Nonfiction

Thomas Conklin
The Titanic Sinks!

Elizabeth Cody Kimmel
Balto and the Great Race

For more great reading ideas,
visit the Random House Web site at
www.randomhouse.com/kids